CROWS AND OWLS

A COLONY OF CROWS DWELT *IN A* GREAT BANYAN TREE IN A FOREST. THE NAME OF THEIR KING WAS CLOUDY.

THE CROWS WERE CONSTANTLY HARASSED BY THEIR POWERFUL ENEMIES, THE OWLS. THEIR KING, FOE-CRUSHER WOULD ATTACK ANY CROW HE CAME ACROSS.

WHOOO-OOOO-IT!

THEN ONE DAY, CLOUDY CALLED A MEETING OF HIS FIVE COUNSELLORS.

THE OWLS ARE BECOMING A MENACE.

THEY ARE ARROGANT AND POWERFUL AND THEY ATTACK US AT NIGHT WHEN WE CANNOT SEE. WE CANNOT COUNTER-ATTACK DURING THE DAY BECAUSE WE DON'T KNOW WHERE THEY DWELL.

ADVISE ME, COUNSELLORS. WHAT SHOULD WE DO?

THEN CLOUDY TURNED TO A VERY OLD CROW NAMED LIVE-STRONG.

AND WHAT DO YOU ADVISE, REVERED SIR?

I ADVISE DUPLICITY, MY LORD.

ATTACK ME AT ONCE WITH A GREAT SHOW OF ANGER.

ATTACK YOU? MY WISEST MINISTER?

YES. WE MUST PUT UP THIS SHOW FOR THE BENEFIT OF OUR FRIEND OVER THERE.

AN OWL!

LET HIM THINK WE'VE FALLEN OUT. THROW ME OUT OF THE TREE. THEN, WITH ALL YOUR SUBJECTS...

...FLY TO ANTELOPE MOUNTAIN.

AND WHAT WILL YOU DO?

I WILL BEFRIEND THE OWLS AND WIN THEIR TRUST. AND THEN I'LL FIND A WAY TO BRING ABOUT THEIR DOOM.

THE OWL LOST NO TIME IN REPORTING WHAT HE HAD HEARD AND SEEN TO HIS MASTER, KING FOE-CRUSHER.

YOUR MAJESTY, THE CROWS ARE FIGHTING AMONGST THEMSELVES.

THEY HAVE THROWN OUT ONE OF THEIR MINISTERS.

THEN THIS IS A GOOD TIME TO ATTACK THEM. A DISORGANISED ENEMY IS EASILY DEFEATED.

FOLLOW ME, MY FRIENDS.

FOE-CRUSHER AND HIS OWLS ATTACKED THE BANYAN TREE WITH BLOODCURDLING WAR CRIES.

WHOOOO!

WHOOO-IEEEE!

BUT THEY SOON REALISED THAT THERE WAS NOT A SINGLE CROW IN THE TREE.

THE COWARDS HAVE FLED!

OLD LIVE-STRONG WHO HAD BEEN WATCHING THE PROCEEDINGS FROM THE GROUND WAS PLEASED WITH THE WAY THINGS WERE GOING.

THE FIRST PART OF MY PLAN HAS SUCCEEDED.

NEXT COMES THE MOST DANGEROUS PART... BUT THERE'S NO TURNING BACK NOW.

WELL, HERE GOES.

CAW! CAW!

LOOK, A CROW!

I AM NO ORDINARY CROW. I AM CLOUDY'S MINISTER. BE GOOD ENOUGH TO INFORM YOUR MASTER OF MY PRESENCE.

I HAVE MUCH TO DISCUSS WITH HIM.

I'LL FETCH HIM.

THE OWL SOON RETURNED WITH FOE-CRUSHER WHO WAS ASTONISHED TO SEE THE BATTERED CONDITION OF THE OLD CROW.

HOW HAVE YOU COME TO SUCH A SORRY STATE, MY DEAR SIR?

THIS IS THE WAY I HAVE BEEN REWARDED FOR GIVING GOOD ADVICE, YOUR MAJESTY.

MY MASTER, CLOUDY, BECAME FURIOUS WITH ME WHEN I URGED HIM TO PAY YOU TRIBUTE. HE ASSAULTED ME AND THREW ME OUT OF THE TREE.

HENCEFORTH I SHALL WORK FOR THE DESTRUCTION OF ALL CROWS. NOW I THROW MYSELF AT YOUR MERCY.

I WILL TALK IT OVER WITH MY ADVISERS.

FOE-CRUSHER HAD FIVE ANCESTRAL COUNSELLORS. THEIR NAMES WERE RED-EYE, FIERCE-EYE, HOOK-NOSE, FLAME-EYE AND WALL-EAR.

THE CROW SEEKS ASYLUM. WHAT IS YOUR OPINION, RED-EYE?

SLAY HIM WITHOUT FURTHER DELAY, MY LORD. HE IS A CROW!

BUT THE OTHER COUNSELLORS WERE MORE CHARITABLE.

GRANT HIM REFUGE, O KING!

IT WOULD BE WRONG TO KILL ONE WHO SEEKS YOUR PROTECTION.

HE MAY PROVE USEFUL TO US IN OUR WAR WITH THE CROWS.

DO NOT LISTEN TO THEM, YOUR MAJESTY. SLAY HIM! HE IS UP TO NO GOOD!

I HAVE ALREADY MADE UP MY MIND, RED-EYE. THE CROW STAYS WITH US. WE SHALL TAKE HIM TO OUR FORTRESS.

THE OWLS LIFTED UP LIVE-STRONG AND CARRIED HIM TO THEIR FORTRESS.

I HAVE FOOLED THEM ALL EXCEPT THE SHREWD RED-EYE. HE HAS GUESSED MY TRUE PURPOSE.

THIS IS OUR FORTRESS, SIR. HERE YOU MAY STAY IN COMFORT AND HONOUR.

HO, THERE! MAKE OUR GUEST COMFORTABLE. LOOK AFTER HIS NEEDS.

IF I STAY IN THEIR MIDST IT WILL BE DIFFICULT FOR ME TO GO ABOUT MY BUSINESS WITHOUT BEING OBSERVED.

O KING, IT WOULD NOT BE PROPER FOR ME TO ENTER YOUR FORTRESS. I AM, AFTER ALL, A CROW AND UNWORTHY OF THE HONOUR.

GIVE ME A LITTLE PLACE NEAR THE GATE AND THAT IS ENOUGH.

YOU MAY STAY NEAR THE GATE IF IT PLEASES YOU, MY FRIEND.

THE SECOND PART OF MY PLAN HAS GONE THROUGH SUCCESSFULLY. I CAN COME AND GO AS I WISH.

LIVE-STRONG MADE HIMSELF COMFORTABLE NEAR THE GATE AND BEGAN TO ENJOY A LIFE OF EASE AND COMFORT, UNPERTURBED BY RED-EYE'S HOSTILITY.

HAVE SOME RICE, YOUR HONOUR.

AND HERE ARE SOME MANGOES.

HOW THEY PAMPER HIM. IT MAKES ME SICK!

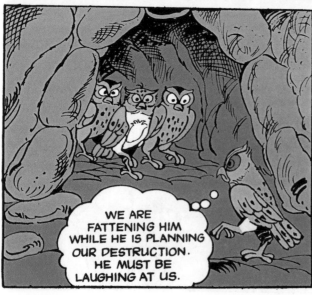

WE ARE FATTENING HIM WHILE HE IS PLANNING OUR DESTRUCTION. HE MUST BE LAUGHING AT US.

YOUR MAJESTY, THE CROW MUST GO! HE IS MAKING A FOOL OF YOU!

RED-EYE!

LEAVE THAT POOR CREATURE ALONE. HE IS HARMLESS.

THEY WON'T LISTEN TO ME. I CAN'T STAY HERE ANY LONGER.

RED-EYE GATHERED HIS FOLLOWERS AND TOLD THEM TO PACK UP THEIR BELONGINGS.

THE END IS AT HAND. I CANNOT SAVE THE KING AS HE REFUSES TO BE GUIDED BY ME. LET US, AT LEAST, SAVE OUR-SELVES WHILE WE CAN.

ANYONE WHO CONTINUES TO LIVE HERE DOES SO AT HIS OWN PERIL. LET US GO FORTH AND SEEK ANOTHER FORTRESS IN THE MOUNTAINS.

LIVE-STRONG WAS OVERJOYED WHEN HE SAW RED-EYE LEAVING THE FORTRESS WITH HIS FOLLOWERS.

ONLY HE COULD HAVE FOILED MY PLANS. THE REST OF THEM ARE NUMSKULLS.

THE DAYS OF THE OWLS ARE NUMBERED. FROM TOMORROW I SHALL START BUILDING MY NEST OF DEATH.

EACH DAY THEREAFTER, LIVE-STRONG WENT INTO THE FOREST AND RETURNED WITH A TWIG WHICH HE DROPPED INSIDE THE GATE.

I AM BUILDING A NEST, YOUR MAJESTY. I HOPE YOU DO NOT MIND.

OF COURSE, NOT!

LET US KNOW IF YOU NEED ANY HELP.

SOON THERE WAS A LARGE PILE OF TWIGS AT THE GATE, BUT NONE OF THE OWLS STOPPED TO WONDER WHY THEIR GUEST REQUIRED SO BIG A NEST.

THEN ONE MORNING WHEN THE OWLS WERE ASLEEP, LIVE-STRONG QUIETLY LEFT THE FORTRESS.

HE FLEW DIRECTLY TO A NEARBY MOUNTAIN WHERE CLOUDY AND THE OTHER CROWS WERE WAITING FOR HIM.

WE ARE DELIGHTED TO SEE YOU BACK WITH US!

AND SOON—

FIRE! THE CAVE IS ON FIRE!

THE OWLS, STILL HALF ASLEEP, TRIED TO RUSH OUT OF THE CAVE BUT WERE BEATEN BACK BY THE FLAMES.

THE CROW HAS DONE THIS! I SHOULD HAVE LISTENED TO MY FAITHFUL RED-EYE!

WE ARE DOOMED! DOOMED!

AH!

THE CAVE, CLOSED AS IT WAS FROM ALL SIDES, BECAME A FIERY FURNACE.

THOSE OF THE OWLS WHO MANAGED TO EVADE THE FLAMES WERE SUFFOCATED BY THE FUMES. ALL OF THEM, INCLUDING KING FOE-CRUSHER, PERISHED.

AND THUS DID THE CROWS RID THEMSELVES OF THEIR POWERFUL BUT DIM-WITTED ENEMIES, THE OWLS.

THE NOBLE ENEMY

A MAN WAS SEARCHING FOR GEMS ON THE TOP OF A CERTAIN MOUNTAIN.

AFTER A LONG UNSUCCESSFUL SEARCH, HE WAS EXHAUSTED AND THREW HIMSELF ON THE GROUND BEHIND A ROCK.

I'LL TAKE A SHORT NAP AND THEN TRY AGAIN.

BZZ...BZZ...BZZ...

...TOO MANY DACOITS AROUND HERE...

...THE GEMS...

GOOD GOD! THOSE YOUNG MEN HAVE FOUND SOME GEMS!

...WOULD BE SAFEST... IN OUR STOMACHS!

THEY ARE SWALLOWING THEM!

THIS IS NOT FAIR AT ALL. I SHOULD GET SOME GEMS TOO FOR MY TROUBLE.

I KNOW WHAT! I'LL MAKE FRIENDS WITH THESE FELLOWS AND WHEN THEY ARE ASLEEP, I'LL SLIT OPEN THEIR BELLIES AND TAKE THE GEMS.

LOOK, THERE'S A MAN FOLLOWING US.

GOOD MASTERS, I AM FORTUNATE TO HAVE MET YOU.

I AM ALONE AND I WAS LOOKING FOR COMPANY ON THIS DANGEROUS ROAD.

YOU ARE WELCOME TO TRAVEL WITH US, MY FRIEND.

THE MORE, THE MERRIER.

GOOD. THEY DON'T SUSPECT ANYTHING.

NOW ALL I HAVE TO DO IS WAIT FOR THE RIGHT MOMENT.

BUT UNFORTUNATELY FOR HIM, THAT MOMENT WAS NEVER TO COME. FOR AS THEY PASSED A VILLAGE THAT LAY ALONG THEIR ROUTE...

...A BIRD IN A ROBBER CHIEF'S HUT BEGAN TO SING.

THEY HAVE GEMS WITH THEM...THEY HAVE GEMS...

GEMS!

SEIZE THOSE MEN! BRING THEM HERE!

THE THREE FRIENDS AND THEIR COMPANIONS WERE CAPTURED AND BROUGHT BEFORE HIM.

I KNOW YOU HAVE GEMS WITH YOU. HAND THEM OVER.

WHAT! GEMS?

SEARCH THEM!

THE MEN SEARCHED THEIR CAPTIVES THOROUGHLY.

THERE HAS BEEN SOME MISTAKE. WE DON'T HAVE ANY GEMS WITH US!

WE CAN'T FIND ANYTHING ON THEM, CHIEF.

HOW'S THAT!

OH, WELL! THE BIRD MUST HAVE BEEN MISTAKEN.

ALL RIGHT. LET THEM GO.

BUT AS SOON AS THEY LEFT, THE BIRD BEGAN TO SING THE SAME SONG AGAIN.

THEY HAVE GEMS WITH THEM... THEY HAVE GEMS WITH THEM...

WHAT! HAVE THEY DECEIVED ME, THEN?

ON THE OTHER HAND, THEY MAY CUT ME FIRST. EITHER WAY I AM DOOMED.

BUT I COULD SAVE THE OTHER FELLOWS. LET ME TRY...

YOU WON'T FIND ANY GEMS IN OUR STOMACHS, SIR. BUT IF YOU INSIST ON SEEING FOR YOURSELF LET ME BE THE FIRST TO DIE.

IT WOULD BE UNBEARABLE FOR ME TO WATCH THE STOMACHS OF MY FRIENDS BEING CUT OPEN.

WHETHER YOU DIE FIRST OR LAST MAKES NO DIFFERENCE TO ME.

TAKE HIM AWAY AND GRANT HIM HIS WISH.

THANK YOU.

IF MY LITTLE TRICK WORKS, MY DEATH WILL NOT HAVE BEEN IN VAIN.

THE MAN WAS TAKEN AWAY. LATER ~

THERE WASN'T A SINGLE GEM IN HIS STOMACH.

WHAT!

SO MY BIRD CAN MAKE A MISTAKE AFTER ALL.

THERE WERE NO GEMS IN HIS STOMACH. THERE WON'T BE ANY IN THE STOMACHS OF HIS FRIENDS EITHER.

THERE HAS BEEN A TERRIBLE MISTAKE, MY FRIENDS. I AM SORRY THAT YOUR COMRADE IS DEAD.

YOU MAY GO.

LITTLE DID THE CHIEF REALISE THAT HE HAD DONE EXACTLY WHAT THE DEAD MAN HAD HOPED HE WOULD DO.

THE FRIENDS TOO, UNAWARE THAT THEY HAD BEEN SAVED BY A CLEVER RUSE, THOUGHT THEY HAD JUST BEEN VERY LUCKY, AND LOST NO TIME IN GETTING OUT OF THE VILLAGE.

MORAL: A SENSIBLE ENEMY CAN OFTEN PROVE TO BE YOUR BEST FRIEND.

THE BIRD AND THE MONKEYS

ONE CHILLY WINTER EVENING—

BRRR—RRR... IT'S COLD.

LOOK, BROTHER! A SPARK OF FIRE.

IT WAS A GLOW-WORM GOING PAST.

I'VE GOT IT!

PUT IT UNDER THIS PILE OF LEAVES.

WE WILL SOON HAVE A BIG BLAZING FIRE TO KEEP OURSELVES WARM.

YOU ARE MAKING A MISTAKE, GOOD SIRS.

THAT'S A FIREFLY YOU'VE CAUGHT...

...NOT A SPARK OF FIRE.

IGNORE HER!

LET'S BLOW ON THE LEAVES. THEY'LL CATCH FIRE FASTER THAT WAY.

LISTEN TO ME, SIRS...

...YOU ARE WASTING YOUR TIME AND ENERGY.

YOU CAN'T SET ANYTHING ALIGHT WITH A FIREFLY.

WHY DON'T YOU...

...STOP PESTERING US, YOU STUPID CREATURE!

DON'T TRY TO TEACH US HOW TO LIGHT A FIRE!

COME ON BROTHERS, LET'S GET BACK TO THE TASK.

PHOOOO!

PHOOOOOO!

MORAL: DON'T TRY TO TEACH THOSE WHO CANNOT BE TAUGHT.

THE CAMEL WHO WAS BEGUILED BY HIS COMPANIONS

A MERCHANT WAS LEADING A CARAVAN OF HEAVILY-LADEN CAMELS THROUGH A JUNGLE...

...WHEN ONE OF THEM, OVERCOME BY FATIGUE, COLLAPSED.

LET US SHIFT HIS LOAD ONTO THE OTHERS AND BE OFF. WE MUST NOT LET THIS LAZY CREATURE DELAY US.

LATER, WHEN THE CAMEL RECOVERED HIS STRENGTH —

THEY HAVE GONE! AND I AM ALONE IN THIS STRANGE JUNGLE.

FORTUNATELY, THERE'S PLENTY OF GRASS HERE. AT LEAST I WON'T STARVE.

DAYS PASSED AND THE CAMEL SOMEHOW SURVIVED THE PERILS OF THE JUNGLE.

THEN ONE DAY, A LION FOLLOWED BY A LEOPARD, A JACKAL AND A CROW, CAME BY.

MY GOD! WHAT STRANGE CREATURE IS THAT!

THAT IS A CAMEL, O KING.

THEY ARE NOT USUALLY FOUND IN JUNGLES.

LET US FIND OUT WHAT HE IS DOING HERE.

WHEN THE CAMEL TOLD THEM HIS STORY—

POOR FELLOW! HE HAS BEEN TREATED VERY BADLY.

YOU HAVE NOTHING TO FEAR NOW, MY FRIEND. HENCEFORTH YOU ARE UNDER MY PROTECTION. COME WITH US.

SO THE CAMEL JOINED THE LION'S ENTOURAGE AND WAS HAPPY TO HAVE FOUND SUCH A STRONG PROTECTOR.

BUT ONE DAY THE LION WAS WOUNDED IN A COMBAT WITH AN ELEPHANT. HE HAD TO RETIRE TO HIS CAVE AND THERE HE REMAINED FOR SEVERAL DAYS...

...MUCH TO THE DISMAY OF THE CROW, THE JACKAL AND THE LEOPARD WHO DEPENDED ON HIM FOR FOOD.

NO MEAT TODAY EITHER.

WE'LL STARVE TO DEATH AT THIS RATE.

THEY LOOK SO SAD. THEY MUST BE WORRYING ABOUT MY HEALTH. I WISH I COULD FEED THEM AS ALWAYS.

I AM SORRY I CANNOT PROVIDE YOU WITH FOOD NOW, MY FRIENDS. I AM TOO WEAK TO HUNT.

YOU WILL HAVE TO FEND FOR YOURSELVES TILL I RECOVER.

WHAT ARE YOU SAYING, MASTER?

HOW COULD WE EVEN THINK OF EATING WHEN YOU ARE STARVING!

THE LION WAS PLEASED WITH THE JACKAL'S REPLY.

YOU HAVE SHOWN YOURSELVES TO BE LOYAL SERVANTS. GO AND ROUND UP AN ANIMAL AND DRIVE IT THIS WAY SO THAT I MAY KILL IT FOR FOOD.

THE JACKAL AND HIS FRIENDS SCOURED THE JUNGLE BUT COULD NOT FIND ANY ANIMAL.

FINALLY, THEY FOUND THEMSELVES BACK WHERE THEY HAD STARTED.

THERE'S REALLY... ...NO NEED... TO EXERT OURSELVES LIKE THIS.

WHAT ELSE CAN WE DO?

WELL, THERE'S THE CAMEL. HIS FLESH COULD SUSTAIN US ALL FOR SEVERAL DAYS.

FORGET IT. THE KING WILL NEVER HURT ANY ANIMAL THAT IS UNDER HIS PROTECTION.

I'LL HAVE A WORD WITH HIM IN ANY CASE.

O KING, WE COULD NOT FIND AN ANIMAL FOR YOU. BUT THERE'S NO NEED FOR YOU TO STARVE.

YOU CAN EAT THE CAMEL.

WHAT!

ARE YOU SUGGESTING THAT I HURT AN ANIMAL THAT IS UNDER MY PROTECTION?

GET OUT OF MY SIGHT, YOU WRETCH!

PLEASE DON'T MISUNDERSTAND ME, O KING.

I WAS ONLY THINKING OF YOUR WELFARE. OUR OWN LIVES ARE WORTHLESS WHEN YOURS IS AT STAKE.

I KNOW IT WOULD BE WRONG FOR YOU TO HURT THE CAMEL IN ORDINARY CIRCUMSTANCES.

BUT WHAT IF HE HIMSELF DEVOTEDLY OFFERED HIS FLESH TO YOU? THEN NO ONE COULD BLAME YOU FOR SLAYING HIM.

I SUPPOSE YOU ARE RIGHT.

IF THE CAMEL WERE TO MAKE SUCH AN OFFER I MIGHT ACCEPT IT.

THE WILY JACKAL RAN BACK TO HIS FRIENDS WHO HAD NOW BEEN JOINED BY THE CAMEL.

FRIENDS, OUR KING IS DYING OF STARVATION. LET US GO AND BEG HIM TO EAT ONE OF US.

IT IS THE LEAST WE CAN DO FOR SUCH A NOBLE SOUL.

WHAT IS IT, MY FRIENDS? HAVE YOU CAUGHT ANY CREATURE?

NO, O KING. WE WERE NOT ABLE TO CATCH ANY CREATURE. YOU MAY EAT ANY ONE OF US INSTEAD.

AND THAT ONE WILL BE THE CAMEL!

I HOPE BROTHER LEOPARD TOO, CATCHES ON!

EAT ME, MASTER AND PROLONG YOUR LIFE FOR A DAY.

NO, NO, YOU'RE TOO SMALL. THE MASTER'S HUNGER WOULD HARDLY BE APPEASED BY EATING YOU.

EAT ME, MASTER.

AS IF YOU'RE VERY BIG YOURSELF.

IT IS ME YOU SHOULD EAT, MASTER.

ALL OF THEM HAVE OFFERED TO LAY DOWN THEIR LIVES FOR THE KING, BUT HE HAS NOT HURT ANY OF THEM.

NOW LET ME TOO MAKE A NOBLE GESTURE. THEY'LL PROTECT ME TOO!

SO THE POOR CAMEL STEPPED FORWARD.

STAND ASIDE, FRIEND LEOPARD. HOW CAN THE MASTER EAT YOU? YOU AND HE BELONG TO THE SAME FAMILY — WELL ALMOST.

EAT ME, MASTER.

AN OMINOUS SILENCE GREETED THE CAMEL'S OFFER. THEN—

I ACCEPT YOUR OFFER, O NOBLE CAMEL.

WHA...?!

BEFORE THE CAMEL COULD GET OVER HIS SHOCK, THE THREE ANIMALS RUSHED AT HIM...

...AND KILLED HIM. THUS DID THREE ROGUES TAKE ADVANTAGE OF THE TRUST REPOSED IN THEM BY A COMRADE.

MORAL: WATCH YOUR STEP WITH FALSE FRIENDS.

The High
and The Mighty

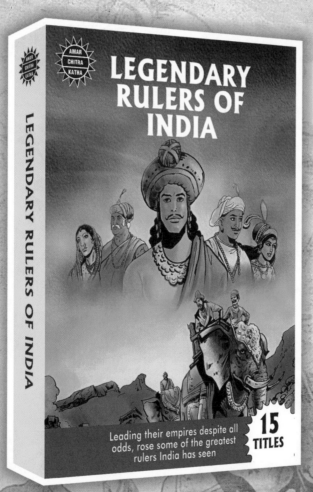

MRP
₹999/-

A gripping account of the life and times of some of the greatest kings the country has ever seen. Legendary Rulers of India features 15 intriguing titles that narrate the forging of India's identity as a great, united nation.